ORLANDO

the Brave Vulture

by Tomi Ungerer

HARPER & ROW, PUBLISHERS NEW YORK

To Jennifer

ORLANDO THE BRAVE VULTURE
Copyright © 1966 by Tomi Ungerer
 For information address Harper & Row, Publishers, Incorporated, 49 East 33rd Street, New York, N.Y. 10016.

Library of Congress Catalog Card Number: 66-12532

Orlando was a Mexican vulture.

One day as he was flying over the desert
he came upon the body of a lost gold miner.

Among the man's belongings he found a picture of the miner's wife and son. There was nothing Orlando could do for him, so he tied up the various objects in a bandanna and flew off.

The first man he met was a poor farmer who could not read.

The farmer led him to the nearest police station.
"Those papers belonged to an American," the officer explained,
"but I don't understand the language.
Our schoolteacher will know where to send them."

The teacher, who read English, was very helpful.
“This is the passport of Nestor Nash,
who comes from Prattleborough, Vermont, in the United States.”

She showed Orlando where it was on a huge globe of the world.
They addressed the bundle, tied it around Orlando's neck, and sent him off.
The valiant vulture flew day and night.

Mrs. Nash had had no word from her husband for a long time.
"This bird must bring a message from your father,"
she said to her son, Finley.
Unfolding the map in the bundle, Finley cried,
"This must be where Daddy is!"
"I wonder if these strange rocks could be the gold Nestor was searching for!" Mrs. Nash exclaimed.

Finley took Orlando to a luncheonette,
and treated him to milkshakes and raw hamburger.

The next day they sold the gold nuggets
to the local jeweler.
"Now we have enough money to search for your father,"
said Mrs. Nash.
And they boarded the next boat to Mexico.

S.S. TORTILLA

In Mexico they shopped for all the equipment they would need for their expedition into the wild desert country.

Following the map's directions, they started their trip.

One night as they rested at a lonely inn
a prowling bandit overheard them talking about the gold mine.

"The little gringo knows where the gold is," he reported to his partner. "Let's kidnap him and he will show us the place."

The plan was quickly executed. Poor Finley was grabbed out of bed, muffled in a serape, and carried away at a gallop.

Next morning when Orlando woke up, he noticed his friend's disappearance, and set off to find him. He soon caught up with the kidnappers.

Scooping up a rock,
he swiftly dropped it on one bandit's head,
then dived for the other.

Clutching Finley in his claws, he soared into the sky.
The other bandit started shooting. Orlando was winged.

Despite his wound, Orlando flew on until he sighted an Indian village.

He landed exhausted. The villagers gathered around Finley
and his feathered rescuer.
"This boy is a gringo," a village elder said.
"The sick one in the hut will know what to do with him."

"Daddy!" screamed the boy when he recognized his father.
"Oh, Finley," said Mr. Nash, "I never thought I'd see you again, until these kind Indians found me half dead in the desert. They brought me here and took care of me."

After Orlando's wing had mended, he was dispatched with a letter to Mrs. Nash. The desperate woman was overjoyed to learn that both Finley and his father were safe.

Mr. Nash repaid the Indians for their kindness by sharing his gold with them. They worked together and the village prospered.

Orlando stayed on
as Finley's pet,
and became
the only beloved vulture
in all Mexico.